# THE
# Mother's Day
# Sandwich

*story by Jillian Wynot* ◆ *pictures by Maxie Chambliss*

ORCHARD BOOKS·NEW YORK

Orchard Books, 387 Park Avenue South, New York, NY 10016

Manufactured in the United States of America. Printed by General Offset Company, Inc.
Bound by Horowitz/Rae. Book design by Mina Greenstein. The text of this book is set in
18 pt. ITC Gamma Book. The illustrations are pencil and pastel drawings, reproduced in halftones.
10  9  8  7  6  5  4  3  2

Library of Congress Cataloging-in-Publication Data
Wynot, Jillian. The Mother's Day Sandwich / by Jillian Wynot ; illustrated by Maxie Chambliss.
p.   cm. "A Richard Jackson book"—P.   Summary: Ivy and Hackett's plan to give their mother a
Mother's Day breakfast in bed almost turns to disaster until Mother finds a way to save the day.
ISBN 0-531-05857-3.   ISBN  0-531-08457-4 (lib. bdg.)   [1. Mother's Day—Fiction.
2. Breakfasts—Fiction.]   I. Chambliss, Maxie, ill.   II. Title.   PZ7.W43636Mo   1990
[E]—dc20   89-35649   CIP   AC

For Stacia and Zachary, with love.
— J.W.


For Carol, at last.
— M.C.

"Get up, Hackett," said Ivy. "It's Mother's Day.
We have to make a surprise for Mama."
"Prize?" said Hackett.

"Yes," said Ivy. "We're making her breakfast in bed."
Hackett followed Ivy into the kitchen.

"Hmm," said Ivy. "What should we make?"
"Cake?" said Hackett.

"No, silly" said Ivy. "We're not allowed to use the oven."

"Egg?" said Hackett.

"No," said Ivy. "I can't turn the eggbeater
and hold the bowl at the same time.

It would dance all around
and fall off the counter and smash.

Besides, we would still need the stove."

Hackett opened the refrigerator. "Fruit?"

Ivy looked at the honeydew. "We'd need a sharp knife," she said.

Hackett took out a jar of mayonnaise.

Ivy frowned. "Put that back, Hackett," she said.
"No one eats mayonnaise plain."
Hackett took out the pickles.
"*Yuck!*" said Ivy.

Hackett took out a stick of butter.
"You are being silly," said Ivy.
Hackett giggled.

"I know," said Ivy. "We'll make cornflakes with milk and a banana. Mama can cut the banana herself. And orange juice."

Hackett smiled.

Ivy climbed up on the counter and opened the cabinet. "Hmm. Maybe the cornflakes are in the back." Out came tuna fish, crackers, coffee and beans, soup, pears, raisins and noodles, jelly, spaghetti, vinegar, tomato sauce, tea, cookies and sardines.

"There they are!" Ivy took down the tall box and poured.

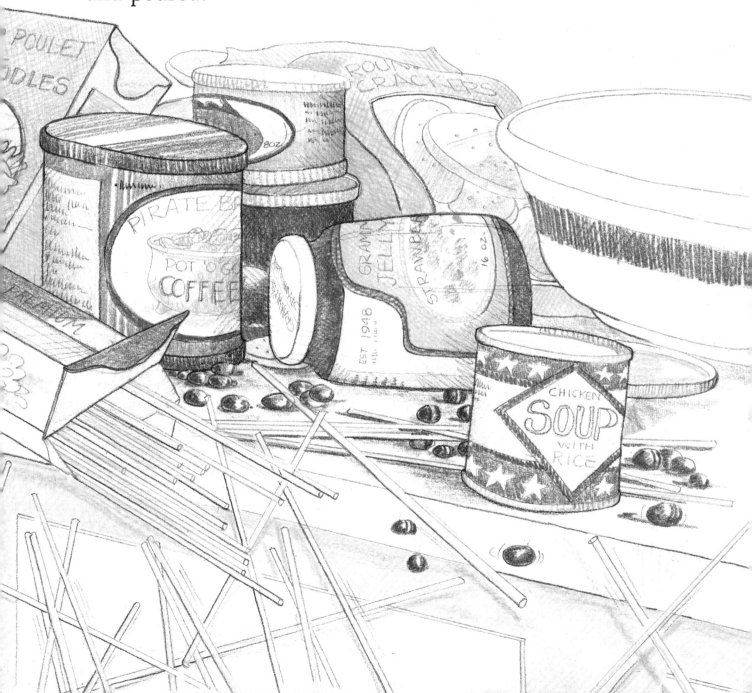

"Oops," she said. "I'll clean those up later."

The milk was too high for Hackett to reach. He
dragged a chair to the refrigerator and climbed up.
He set the container on the chair and climbed down.
*Plop!*

"Oh, Hackett!" Ivy sighed. "We'll mop that up
later. But maybe I should get the orange juice. You
get the banana."

The bananas were stuck together at one end. Hackett tugged and pulled and squeezed, but he couldn't get one loose. He picked up the whole bunch of bananas and thumped them on the table.

"Hackett, *no!*" yelled Ivy. "They'll be all smushed and mushy."

Hackett started to cry.

"Don't cry," said Ivy. "I think there's one that's still good. I'll get the banana. You get the spoon and the knife."

At last, everything was neatly arranged on the tray.

"Ready, Hackett?" asked Ivy.

"Wait," said Hackett. He ran out to the yard. He ran back in with a bunch of yellow buttercups.

"Perfect!" Ivy arranged them in a little pink vase in the center of the tray. Then she held her finger to her lips. "Shh," she said. "Let's be as quiet as mice. We want Mama to be surprised."

They tiptoed to Mama's room.
Mama was fast asleep. Silent as fog, they tiptoed in.

Slowly, Ivy lowered the tray.

Quietly, Hackett unfolded the tray's feet.

Carefully, slowly, quietly, they set the tray down around Mama.

"Now?" whispered Hackett.

"Now!" whispered Ivy.

*"Happy Mother's Day!"* they shouted.

"Wggfcch! *Ughff! Hunh?*" Mama sat up with a jerk.
The tray toppled over. Orange juice and milk, cornflakes
and smushed banana, buttercups and water went flying.
"Oh, my," said Mama. "What's all this?"

Ivy and Hackett started to cry.

"It was supposed to be a surprise," said Ivy. "For Mother's Day."

Mama wiped banana off her nose. "Well, you certainly surprised me," she said, laughing.

Ivy smiled.

Hackett giggled.

"Come here, you two," Mama said. "Do you know what I would really like? A Mother's Day sandwich."

"A sandwich for breakfast?" asked Ivy. "I'll make it."

"No, me!" said Hackett.

Mama pulled them back. "You don't make a
Mother's Day sandwich in the kitchen. You can make
it right here."

"Here?" said Ivy.

"Yes," said Mama. "You be one slice of bread, Ivy.
And Hackett, you be the other slice. And I will be
the cheese."

Hackett and Ivy giggled.

"Now, listen, you two pieces of bread," said Mama.
"Squeeze very close to the cheese, so it can't fall out."

Ivy and Hackett squeezed very close to the cheese.
"Happy Mother's Day," said the two slices of bread.

"Thank you," said the cheese.